Posie the Kitten in Pink

Sarah Phillips · Stua

make believe ideas

D0830703

Posie's the smallest kitten in town.

Her tail is smooth and her paws are round,
but her coat is covered in different patches
of colour and pattern – NOTHING matches!

"I'm a fright," moans Posie, "a terrible sight!
A mix and a mess of black, grey and white,
with splodges and stripes of ginger and brown,
a comical ear and a crazy frown!"

"Don't be depressed," says Midge the Mouse.
"Let's go for a stroll towards my house

and have some fun with the things we find
in the bits and bobs that are left behind."

The friends spy something long and thin,
peeking out of the garbage bin.

Is it a bird?

What could it be?

They decide to set the

creature

free!

They push and shove
and drag and pull
the heavy bin,
but it's too full.

At last it starts to
tip and sway.
Take care!
Keep out of the way!

The pink bird-animal is in a heap.
"Perhaps," says Midge, "it's fast asleep?"

"Maybe," adds Posie,
"we've got it wrong
and it's no animal
but a long, long . . ."

"... SCARF, soft, feathery
and pink!
The colour suits m
don't you think?"

"LOOK HERE!" squeaks Midge.
"Let's try THIS too!
I'm not quite sure what you have to do."
PSHHHHHT!
Pink spray

Wow! Now Posie glitters and glows,
and sparkles from her head to her toes.
Midge stares and can't believe his eyes.
He hops from foot to foot and cries:

"The Kitten in Pink, that's what you are,
a dazzling, beautiful superstar!
All cats will stop and gaze at you
and follow what you say and do!"

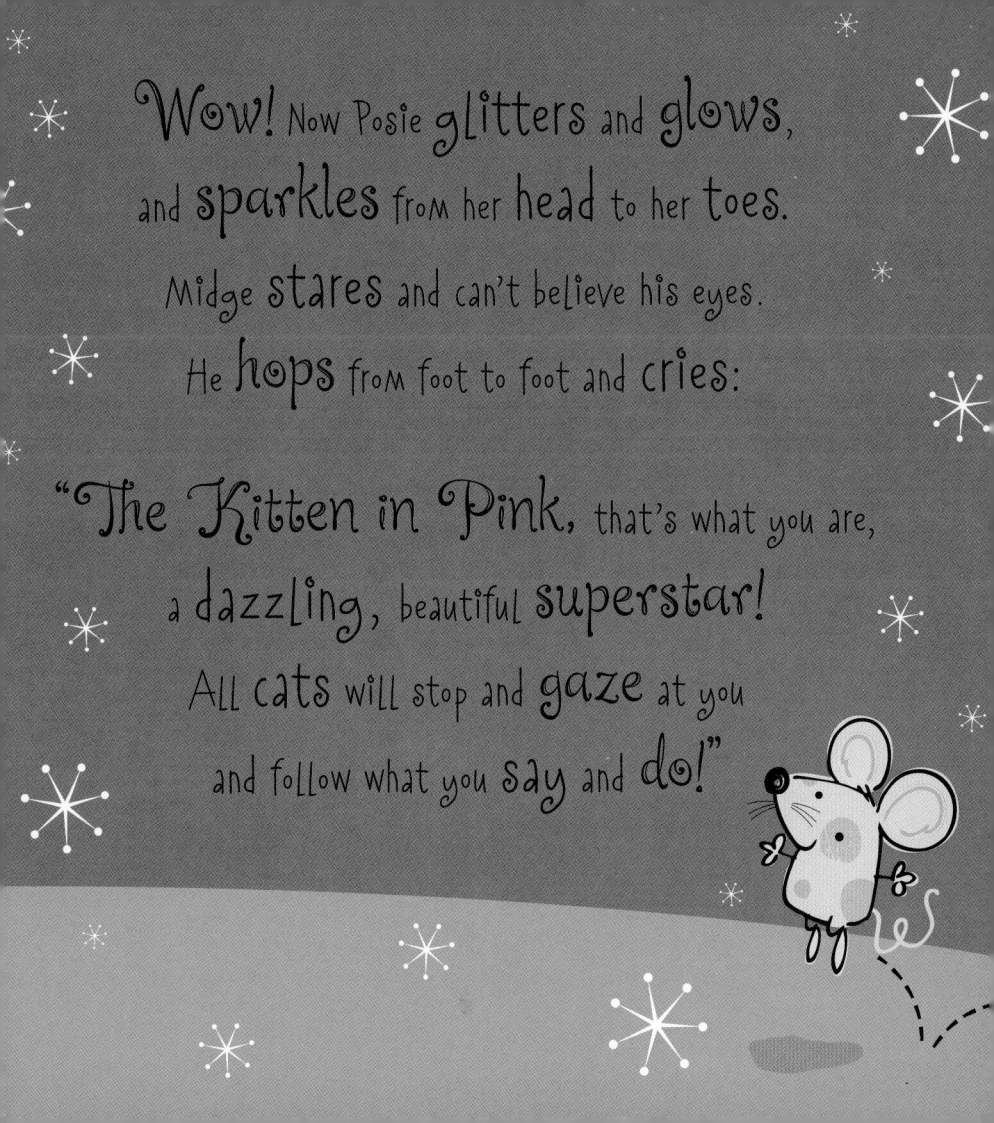

The friends run through the park and see Little Lil by the big oak tree.

"I've lost my rope; I'm all alone.
It's no fun playing on your own!"
BOB'S BAKERY
FRED'S FISH

Posie suggests,
"Let's use my scarf
to help Lil skip
and make her laugh!"

The feathers tickle and Little Lil giggles;
as she skips, she wiggles and wriggles.

They hear a cry as Granny Cat slips
and scatters wool as she trips.
Three naughty kitties want some fun –
they grab the balls and start to run.

"STOP!"

cries Posie, her eyes aflame.

The kitties stare and are filled with shame.
They bring the wool, and feeling sad,
say sorry to Granny for being bad.

Suddenly up run two big cats,
carrying black sacks on their backs.

"Help me, please!" cries Baker Bob.

"My money's gone.

I've been robbed!"

Now Posie thinks and moves at speed;
most keen to help a cat in need.
One thief is caught with
a pink lasso,

ile a woollen web
catches number two.

"To thank you," Bob says, "please do take your pick of any of my cakes."

As they start eating cakes and pies,
big, black rain clouds fill the skies.

Rain washes all the glitter away.
Posie shone pink for one short day,
but she's happy now and will worry less
that her mixed-up coat is a funny mess.

The important thing is what you do,
not whether your coat is pink or blue.
Helping those who are stuck or sad
makes them happy and leaves you glad!